AT THE END OF HOLYROOD LANE

For Mum and the little black dog in Corfu.
— D.P.

For A.J., my safe place in a storm.
— N.J.

First published 2018

EK Books
an imprint of Exisle Publishing Pty Ltd
PO Box 864, Chatswood, NSW 2057, Australia
226 High Street, Dunedin, 9016, New Zealand
www.ekbooks.org

A CiP record for this book is available from the National Library
of Australia.

ISBN 978-1-925335-76-7

Designed by Big Cat Design
Typeset in Lemonade Bold 23 on 24pt
Printed in China

This book uses paper sourced under ISO 14001 guidelines from
well-managed forests and other controlled sources.

10 9 8 7 6 5 4 3 2 1

Endorsed by:

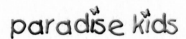

AT THE END OF HOLYROOD LANE

Dimity Powell & Nicky Johnston

Flick lives beneath the beech woods

at the end of Holyrood Lane.

She dances with
butterflies in spring,

tumbles through ruby
leaves in autumn,

and basks in golden
sunshine all year long.

Except when it storms.

Flick never knows when
a squall will strike or
how long it will last.

Whenever angry clouds
muscle in and wild winds
bully the curtains, she
hopes with all her heart
they will just blow over.

But sometimes, no matter
how hard she hopes ...

... it pours and pours.

Storms smother sunshine
and ransack fun.

Sometimes, they roar so
loudly, Flick's ears hurt
and her head throbs.

Storms make Flick feel
smaller than she really is.

So, whenever it's stormy,

Flick hides.

Flick is an expert hider.

She can hide all day ...

and night,

in places where
the thunder
cannot reach her.

But one day, as Flick chases a
rainbow across the antique rug,
around the mahogany dresser,
and down the front steps, a
monstrous storm strikes,

darker and louder than she has ever known.

This time, there is no time to hide.

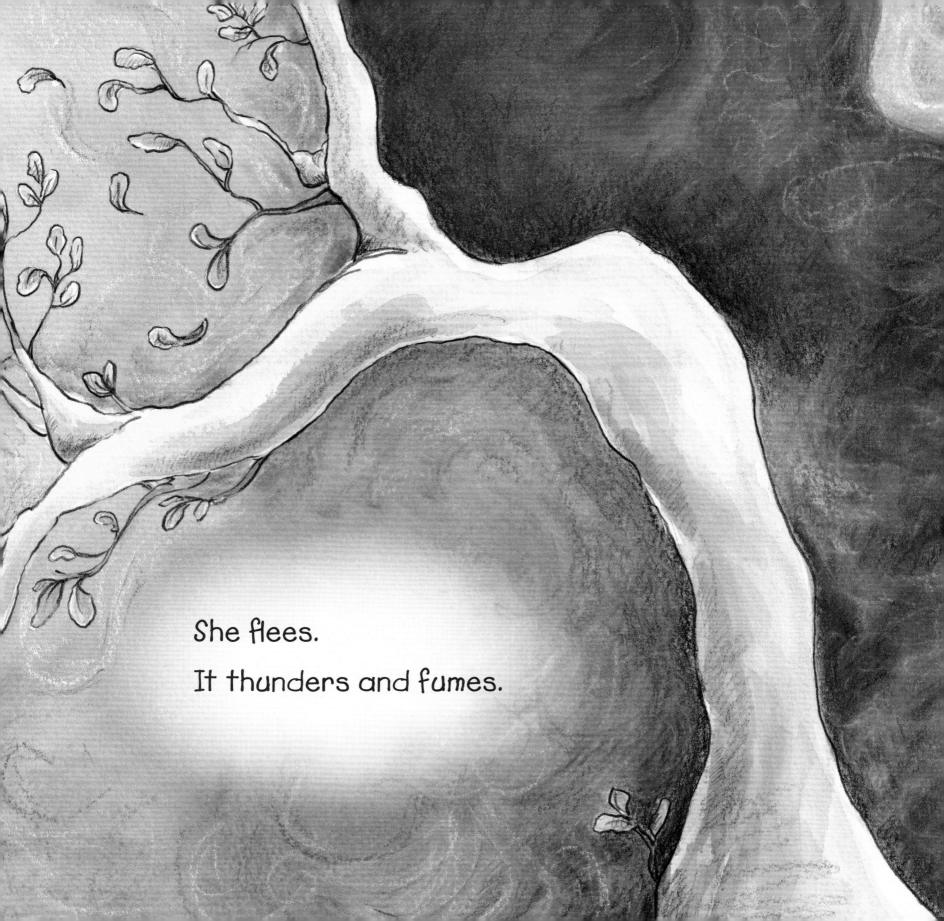

She flees.

It thunders and fumes.

She tries to ignore it.

It bellows and booms.

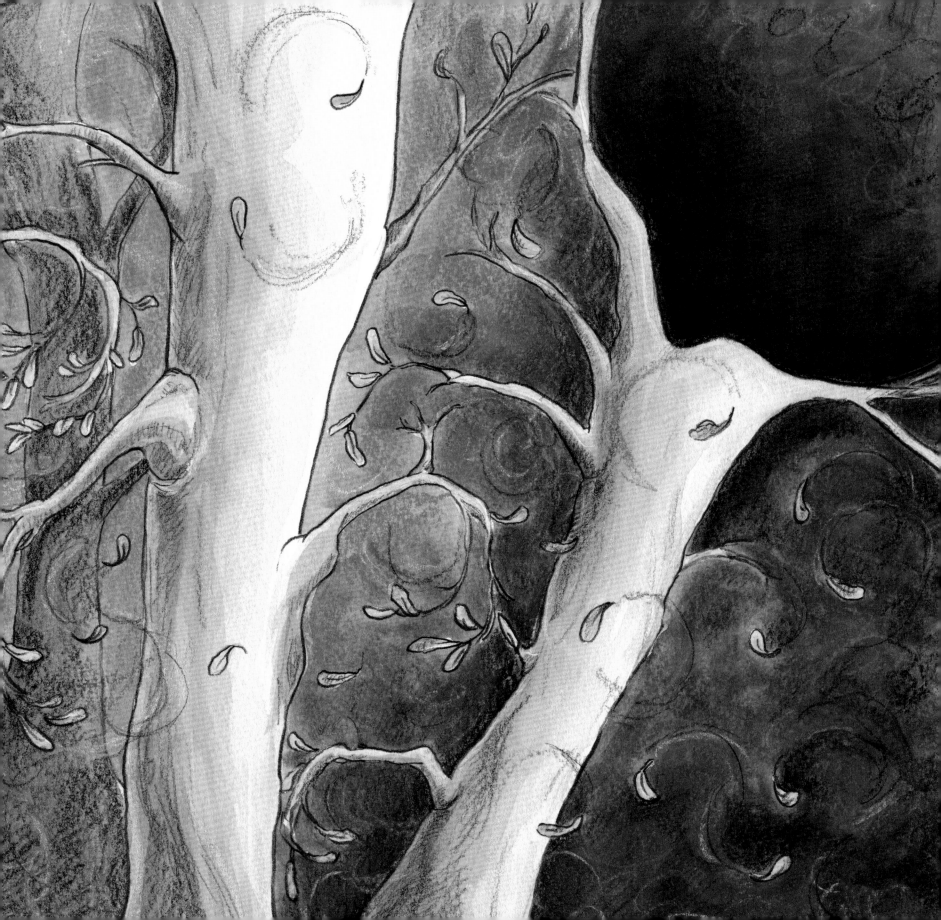

She darts and dodges.

It seethes and snarls,
fiercer and faster,
drenching her in its fury.

Until, sodden and shaken,
Flick does something she
has never done before.

She seeks help.

It works.

After a while and one or two rumbles and grumbles later, the storm leaves ...

and the sun comes out.

A fresh breeze tickles the curtains. Flick hesitates. *Was that the growl of thunder?*

No, there is not a storm cloud in sight.

The breeze ebbs and sunlight melts like butter on her cheeks.

Beneath the towering
beech woods, at the
end of Holyrood Lane,
sunshine spills over
the windowsills ...

and butterflies flit
through the leaves.

Sometimes, it rains.

But it never storms anymore.